Footprint of Troll from Vistavagge 1971

THE TROLL GUIDE

BY ANDERS SKOGLIND

DARK HORSE BOOKS

Purpose of this book

This book is intended for people who want to get the most out of their mountain holiday. To hike and enjoy beautiful mountain scenery and the fresh air is quite good enough, of course, but for the tourist who thirsts for knowledge, there is more to discover. In addition, it can be useful to know, for example, what a Constipation Morel looks like, or where a Hair Troll comes on the Bauer scale. It can actually be crucial to your well-being!

So why are the fungi and trolls in the next pages not already depicted and described in other publications? Few learned men, not least Linnaeus, have visited the mountain world. Why did Linnaeus not write of and categorize these phenomena during his journey in 1732?

Well, he began in his usual way to systematize and note down everything new he saw in nature. Mountain daisies, dwarf birches, and rock lichens were collected, drawn, and archived at a cracking pace, but suddenly he began to find plants *of singular species* which would not fit into cryptogams, phanerogams, or other accepted -gams. He merely scraped the surface of this mystic flora, but what he saw was sufficient for Linnaeus to realize that some features of the mountain world would never let themselves be categorized in his world of order and discipline. He broke off his Lapland journey and made his way back south to continue his work where nature was more predictable.

Linnaeus saw nothing in the way of trolls. By nature they are reserved and often stay away from humans, not because they are afraid of us, but because they do not have the energy to deal with us. They consider themselves superior, of a nobler type... The fact that many of them can make themselves dark, invisible even, did not make things any easier for Linnaeus. Therefore, their existence is questioned even in our enlightened day and age. Not by the people who live and spend time in the mountains, of course. Mountain people know how to avoid trolls. When now and then someone disappears or is eaten, it is usually an inexperienced mountain tourist.

Since I have an educational and popular scientific inclination, I decided to fill the gap in scientific learning which made Linnaeus unsure. My intention is to spread awareness of mountain secrets among the population in general.

Author

Arctic Reverse Dandelion

Knifegnome

Carl Linnaeus

Born on May 13, 1707, in Råshult, Sweden; died on January 10, 1778, in Uppsala.

Author of major works, including *Systema Naturae* and *Species Plantarum*.

Sweden's, and one of the world's, best-known botanists. Also doctor, geologist, pedagogue, ornithologist, and zoologist. Probably good at lots of other things too. Only apparent shortcoming was unwillingness to deal with trolls and other such beings.

Book structure

As you, dear reader, will notice, there is no system in which things are presented in this book.

This is not a flagrant oversight by the author, but totally intentional!

Why? Just bear in mind that there are readers who have no time at all for botany. They would skip an entire section on plants, and thereby risk missing important facts; for example, the fact that one should not consume a Constipation Morel at a banquet.

If the reverse should occur, that the botanists skip the sections on dangerous trolls, the consequences could be dire. Furthermore, it can be overwhelming for the prospective first-time hiker to see page after page of the most frightening apparitions. Perhaps this person would hesitate to visit the mountains, which would be sad. So it can be useful to break things up with fairly harmless members of the plant kingdom amid the riot of repulsive trolls and other beings.

In all other fact-based works, I am a devoted supporter of division into chapters. So I do not wish to start a trend with this, but allow this publication to be the exception that proves the rule.

Personal troll protection

It can be good to know a few things before getting to grips with the study of mystic mountain flora and fauna.

Forget the notion that steel can protect one against trolls in these latitudes. Further south possibly, but the mountains are so rich in ore that the troll is guaranteed to be immune. Nor is a cross as effective in a mountain setting as it apparently is further south. However, the mountain troll does detest the X. This is the single reason why mountain trails are marked with Xs. A so-called "troll cross" considered to provide protection against trolls and goblins is in fact in the form of an X. It further supports this proposition. The expression "RelaaX, maan" is not Jamaican in origin, but is based on the fact that X-marked trails are "peaceful" zones that trolls and goblins prefer to avoid.

The idea that trolls might shy away from steel is questionable. Many trolls are pictured with iron objects on their belt, such as scissors and knives. One can also see pictures in which they have wrought iron bracelets. One theory is that these misconceptions are in fact planted in the human consciousness by trolls. It is a kind of lobbying campaign which has gone on for centuries, aimed to lull us into a false sense of security.

But the most important personal protection is of course to carry a copy of this book in the side pocket of your backpack, or to learn it by heart. Then you can quickly assess the situation in an encounter.

Striking steel

Scissors

Magnetite (iron ore)

How to protect your food

When you know a little more about the fantastic inhabitants of the mountains and what they are capable of, you must sooner or later ask yourself the question: how come the mountain people can have their things undisturbed? How come the trolls do not empty all their small pillar-mounted stores (called *njalla* or *ájtte*) where they keep food and provisions? A troll will of course happily leap at one of them and empty it of anything of value, unless it is protected by runes! Look more closely at an untouched njalla and you will see a row of runic letters on the door or somewhere on the wall. The troll can only futilely shake his hairy fist and curse the miserly njalla owners who do not wish to share the delicacies.

Is it not sufficient to simply paint an X, you may wonder, interferi... attentive reader? Of course, but if you go to the trouble of building such a store and placing food in it, you do of course want to safeguard it as much as possible. The different trolls can require different kinds of protection. Sometimes one can see ancient stone circles around the places to be protected. In that case it is the minerals used that are said to have troll-repellent properties.

Defenseless njalla

The Bauer scale

The origin of this instrument for measuring troll performance is lost in the misty past. But persistent rumors have it that it was written down by some resourceful workers building the inland railway. Other sources state that it is older and has been reworked a number of times.

Yes, it is brief, but in an emergency you do not have time to read a novel, but simply want a good basis for a quick decision, flight or fight.

In general, you can say that trolls are hardy individuals by nature and therefore often put their trust in their muscles. They seldom have weapons, and prefer to grasp the nearest fairly solid object of suitable density and swing it, or throw it at the opponent.

Regarding the properties of trolls

There are of course many different types of troll, but it can be good to know a few things about their physiognomy and properties.

Speed: No troll is exactly quick off the mark, but once they have built up some momentum they can reach speeds that rival the fastest mammals. They also have enormous stamina. Gnormvid of Kärkkevagge is legendary in this context and in his best years could catch up with a stampeding reindeer herd while running backward.

Age: It has not been ascertained how old mountain trolls can be, but it is a fact that there are still living trolls who have met Charles Rabot, the first person to climb the south peak of Kebnekaise in 1883, or Anders Celsius and Maupertuis during the geodesic expedition of 1736. There are even trolls that have met "the first tourist" —Jean-François Regnard, who visited the Kiruna Mountains in 1681. There is more— these are only the verifiable facts.

The Vistavagge Troll, considered one of the oldest in the mountain world, himself claims to have experienced the inland ice. Whether this last claim is in the realm of reality is uncertain, and it is generally considered that the troll in question is prone to exaggerate.

Size: There are trolls that are so big that when they stand up, the landscape changes. These major trolls are often low-intensive and can lie motionless for decades, during which time dense vegetation can take root on the troll. It sounds incredible, but the skin of certain trolls has a tendency to interact with surrounding nature. If a troll falls asleep against the side of a mountain for a decade, its skin becomes stone-like and can barely be distinguished from the surrounding quantities of rock and mineral.

Many people in Kiruna have heard the story of Sten "Burträskaren" Olsson, who found what he thought was a cave. The walls bore traces of copper, but when Sten had swung his mineral hammer a few times, he was sneezed out of a giant troll's nostril.

Strength: The strongest trolls are grotesquely strong, but even an ordinary troll 3.5 m (11.5 ft) in height has the capacity of a small wheel loader. Add to that a long reach and you understand what a pickle you are in if you stray into a dead end where a troll is blocking your way. Whatever the situation, ensure that you have a clear evacuation route.

If contrary to expectations you find all possibilities of flight exhausted, only two alternatives remain. One is to talk your way out of the situation, appealing to the troll's good nature and praising its attractive exterior. Most trolls are extremely vain, so flattery is not as strange as it sounds. Alternative two is to explode in a shower of kicks and blows to send the troll packing. The latter alternative has little prospect of success, even if you possess a belt in Asian martial arts of the very darkest hue.

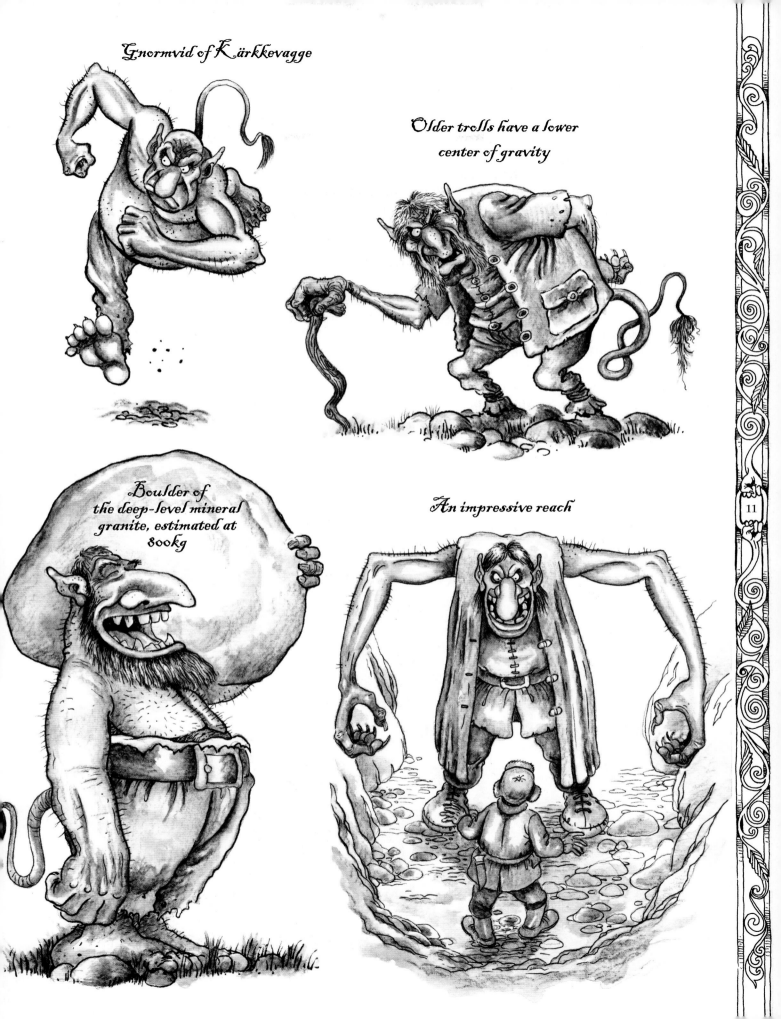

Gnormvid of Kärkkevagge

Older trolls have a lower
center of gravity

Boulder of
the deep-level mineral
granite, estimated at
800kg

An impressive reach

How do you know when it is safe to approach a troll?

Well, if you have not succeeded in identifying the troll, if you do not possess this Troll Guide or quite simply run into an undescribed or unknown life form, common sense goes a long way.

A lot can be learned from the body language. Below, for example, we have a troll which is showing all the signs of a repressed urge to begin fisticuffs. He has adopted a pose which clearly shows that vocal arguments, however presented, are superfluous. A wise wanderer will immediately begin an ordered retreat. The direction is insignificant since the primary need is to get some distance from the troll.

The huge being on the opposite side, however, is often safe to approach. The ancient Vistavagge Troll is kindly disposed to mountain hikers, as long as they pick up their litter and are polite. He often sits leaning against the side of a mountain at the entrance to a valley and likes a chat. He can, however, become rather monotonous, so whoever has met him once will prefer to take a detour into the valley. If many trolls prefer to stay hidden, the social needs of the Vistavagge Troll mean that he, on the other hand, will gladly make himself visible to people. Sometimes, however, he forgets to do this and begins speaking to a person, who looks around in confusion for the owner of the deep voice.

Now, dear hiker, you are better prepared for your mountain tour. Just remember to be aware of your surroundings. Do not turn your back on this stone formation on your way to Kopparåsen. And if you are hiking to Tarfala and make your way past this picturesque waterfall (opposite), then whatever you do, remain alert.

You are now ready to encounter on the pages that follow the trolls that call the mountain world home. Remember! From now on, keep the book packed in a safe but easily accessible place. It is a good idea to practice pulling it out as quickly as possible and leafing through it at a speed that feels comfortable without dropping the book.

Many-headed trolls

The Triple-Headed Terror from Låkkta (on the right) is a hedonistic and terrifying sight. This many-headed and many-armed mountain creature is more devious than a trapped wolverine. He is almost impossible to avoid, since he has good vision due to the three pairs of eyes. The only way to escape is to try to get the three heads to quarrel with each other. A man from Puoltsa managed to do this one spring day in 1988 by suggesting different ways to cook his own wretched body. This method, which is called the "Puoltsa Maneuver," has since then become a standard method to deal with this troll. In more ways than one, a three on the Bauer scale.

The Dual-Headed Sour Troll from Sarek is at least as frightening by nature and appearance as the Låkkta troll. But here it is impossible to fool the two heads into quarreling, since they are already chronically at odds over everything. The only way they agree is typically when they have found something edible. There is no known method to escape the Sour Troll. To crouch and play dead does not work. Kicking and screaming is good advice.

The Wandering Peat Goahti

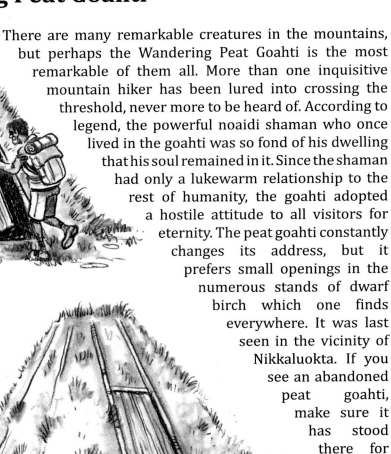

There are many remarkable creatures in the mountains, but perhaps the Wandering Peat Goahti is the most remarkable of them all. More than one inquisitive mountain hiker has been lured into crossing the threshold, never more to be heard of. According to legend, the powerful noaidi shaman who once lived in the goahti was so fond of his dwelling that his soul remained in it. Since the shaman had only a lukewarm relationship to the rest of humanity, the goahti adopted a hostile attitude to all visitors for eternity. The peat goahti constantly changes its address, but it prefers small openings in the numerous stands of dwarf birch which one finds everywhere. It was last seen in the vicinity of Nikkaluokta. If you see an abandoned peat goahti, make sure it has stood there for a while before you peek in.

The chain of events in three stages

The Torneträsk Rascals

They are two old troll brothers who live on the eastern shore of Lake Torneträsk. They are quarrelsome, messy, and noisy. To let off steam, they throw stones at fishing boats. Like many other trolls and beings, they can make themselves invisible. But the fishermen's association has learned over the years how to adapt to the moods of the Torneträsk Rascals and has wisely placed buoys on the lake at roughly the distance trolls can throw large rocks, as a warning to shipping. These beings are dangerous to approach and rated at least three on the Bauer scale. If you are entertaining plans to visit these parts of the lake, it is a good idea to keep handy a pair of occult vision spectacles. These spectacles will be dealt with in a later chapter in this book.

19

The One-Eyed Troll

These trolls are very accident prone. They often step into ravines and cracks in glaciers and so on, since their depth perception is not as good as with two-eyed beings.

They do, however, grow big and strong, and must not be underestimated. They are extremely stubborn, and among mountain people there are occasionally discussions of whether these beings in particular have given rise to the expression "a one-eyed view." They are notorious for failing to see the whole perspective, both literally and practically.

There are few One-Eyed Trolls left in the mountains. If you want to see one, there are nevertheless good opportunities, since like many other trolls they need visual eye contact with any person to whom they wish to make themselves invisible. The Duolbagorni crater is often a good place.

The Mountain Puff Wight

These small green leaf-dwelling wights spend their days in a cloud of smoke that never lifts during the snow-free period. A cautious hiker who enters such a cloud of smoke certainly becomes relaxed and pleased with life, but also eventually unconscious and in possession of a considerable hangover, if the hiker wakes up at all. The "tobacco" for the wights' smoke sticks is made from Mountain Puff, a grass species whose properties in dried, refined condition give the wights a calm, laid-back attitude toward their environment. The wights see the future with confidence and do not disturb their days with any unnecessary chores, apart from lighting up a new smoke stick.

The Constipation Morel

Its unattractive exterior should convince normal people not to taste the fungus. Nonetheless, some mountain hikers always fall for it every year, victims of this intestine-squeezing despot among the mountain flora. One major reason is that to the human eye, the Constipation Morel looks like a tasty chanterelle. The only way to identify the fungus is through a pair of occult spectacles. These spectacles will be dealt with in a later chapter. However, if you do not become suspicious at finding a large chanterelle on a bare mountain and prepare it, the course of the illness is as follows: sudden surprise that the fungus does not taste of chanterelle, then a growing pain in the abdominal region, successively rising to a crescendo after three days. Diarrhea and vomiting become part of everyday life during this period. After a week you are back on your feet, thoroughly uninterested in all forms of fungus.

The Dragon Flap Clover

To the superstitious, a four-leaf clover means luck, happiness, and success. This clover, unfortunately, offers mostly misery. If you touch a leaf, then there is an allergic reaction that makes you sneeze. The sneezing attacks are long and difficult to stop. Furthermore, the skin turns red where it has been in contact with the leaf. Infernally, the itching begins at the same time as the victim begins having sneezing attacks. It is a remarkable spectacle to see someone afflicted by this torment trying to sneeze and scratch at the same time. It is extremely fortunate that the symptoms can be alleviated by cold bathing. Jump into the nearest stream. Just look out for Leviathan Trout and Brook Nymphs. These phenomena will be dealt with in a later chapter.

The Shifty Biff-Bolete

This double-crossing bon vivant hides its arms in the underlying vegetation and bides its time. The fungus knows that sooner or later a bird will land to peck at its mushroom-like head. Then within hundredths of a second it lashes out. The illustration has been drawn in slow motion to clarify the sequence of events in an adequate manner. The formidable speed of the action is without doubt comparable to the wing beats of a hummingbird.

The Mountain Oyster Mushroom

Has similarly sinister properties. Quite cynically gives the impression to insects and creepy-crawlies that here we have a juicy cloudberry to be savored. Instead it is the mushroom that gains some sustenance. To people, this oyster is delicious and rich in vitamins and other beneficial substances. They do, however, take a long time to boil. The "cloudberry" is mineralized and inedible, but can make a nice ornament.

The Smoke Troll

This creature is constantly surrounded by smoke. Many mountain hikers have from a distance mistaken the thick smoke for a brush fire and have hurried there to ascertain the extent of the disaster and to alert the water bombers. But to their amazement they find merely an enormous pillar of smoke with a vegetable fragrance, often above a sittable tree stump. The Smoke Troll himself can only be seen through occult spectacles. These spectacles will be dealt with in a later chapter. The expression "gone up in smoke" probably stems from this. The Smoke Troll gathers Smoking Pipe Moss, which it grinds in a special grinder wrought by dwarfs which treats the moss in an extra-thorough way so that all the aromas benefit the smoker. Of all the inhabitants of the mountains, it is only the Mountain Puff Wights that smoke more than the Smoke Troll in relation to the bodyweight/tobacco volume.

Pouch for tobacco

Tobacco grinder

Smoking Pipe Moss

The Duel Lemming

These armor-clad rodents prompt many questions as they initiate a duel. On the picture, an impartial Snow Hamster is officiating and refereeing. The lemming world comprises different clans, all of them feuding with each other. Challenges and thrown gauntlets are part of everyday life. On average 12 lemmings a day are insulted or affronted. This leads to bloody conflicts and face-offs that sometimes culminate in multiple rodent deaths. The fact that the lemming population is sometimes dramatically reduced has nothing to do with any mass exodus of lemmings.

The armor and weapons are all wrought by dwarfs and therefore of the highest quality. It may seem odd that a rodent species can maintain such a level of understanding and intelligence alongside an irreconcilable attitude to a neighboring clan, but on the other hand there is much that is odd in the mountains. To mountain hikers interested in handicraft there are many details to study in new lemming armor. Old armor tends to be dented...

The Predatory Hare

To be hunted by a band of aggressive and demented hares with fangs is no stroll in the park. On the contrary, it is an unpleasant experience which few have experienced and lived to tell the tale. Like shoals of piranhas, they attack in groups and overwhelm the victim, leaving only white bones and pieces of fabric.

In the 1930s, a British tourist named Heathcliff Wolmerston-Utherridge discovered to his joy that the Predatory Hare does not appreciate tweed. This textile has a tendency to swell in the hare's throat when mixed with its saliva, completely ruining its appetite. So if you intend to undertake a tour in the Rapa Valley, this textile is recommended.

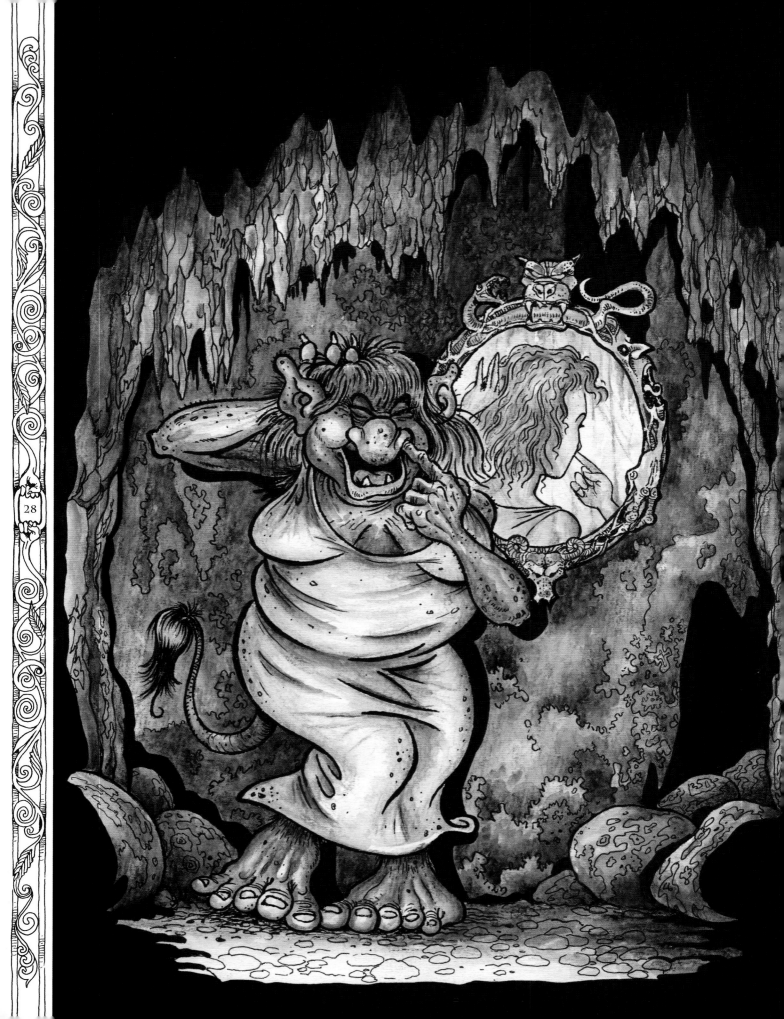

Troll women

Troll women are generally as ugly as the men. There are of course exceptions, but overall it is no exaggeration to call them as ugly as sin. They consider themselves of above-average attractiveness and photogenic. How is this possible? Do they have ample self-confidence as well as a grandiose ego? Yes, but most troll women are also the proud owners of a troll mirror.

It will always show its owner in the best light, in a resplendent light blue nuance. This is in fact the origin of the expression "a blue lie." "The troll mirror" is actually a slightly misleading term, since it is often a product of dwarfs' smithing.

Exceptions

The Barb-Beaked Buzzard

Mating conflicts among these overaggressive buzzards are blood-filled orgies. This giant with a 4 m (13 ft) wingspan is omnivorous when it comes to meat but has a weakness for reindeer.

The bird spreads fear and despondency wherever it goes. Among its good qualities is that the population is small, barely 15 nesting pairs in the entire mountain range. It is in imminent danger of extinction, but nobody is notably upset about this. One known habitat is in the Naymats Massif.

The Dragonback Ptarmigan

A conceited bird! There is no other way to put it, since its crest continues all the way down its back. This ptarmigan has delicious meat, but is difficult to fell. Many consider the species to be associated with the powers of darkness and only a silver bullet can kill it. Furthermore, one might mention that it also goes under the name "the mountain desperado," since its eyes are framed by a black stripe, giving it the appearance of a masked criminal.

The Knife-Tailed Capercaillie

A territorial, elusive roughneck of a bird which raises its young on small trolls and cranberries. The unique tailfeathers merit a 59 on the Rockwell hardness scale and are popular among knifesmiths. There is a theory that the capercaillie's habit of eating gravel, in this case ore-rich pebbles in springtime, together with a metabolic calcifying process, contributes to the hardness of the rather curious feathers. This is asserted by Hilmer Wridmarker, the ornithologist born in Leipojärvi who studied this capercaillie species for many years and has published interesting in-depth articles on the subject.

Hilmer Wridmarker

Female

Barb-Beaked Buzzard

Dragonback Ptarmigan

Knife made from tail feathers

Knife-Tailed Capercaillie

The Flying Fell Dog (Canis pegasus)

This modern-day cousin of the pterodactyl has an impressive wingspan which exceeds even that of the Barb-Beaked Buzzard. That makes it the biggest flying animal in the mountains.

The bird's profile is fearsome and the very sight of it can freeze to ice the blood of even the most hardened and experienced alpinists. As if this were not enough, this hideous creation is also equipped with a penetrating cry that proclaims death and misery where it echoes hauntingly between the mountain massifs. As much as humanly possible, avoid close contact with this bird.

The Crested Raven

Barely bigger than an ordinary raven. It is recognized by its significant double crest which gives it its name. How refreshing with a small harmless bird, you are thinking, dear reader. Unfortunately, its size is misleading, as its many victims have found out. This is an extremely scheming and sinister individual! It pecks at and devours dead and living meat with the same voracious appetite. An individual is certainly manageable, but a flock of Crested Ravens can rout a small army.

The Tarfala Penguin

It is also known as the "Scandinavian Dodo": a wingless bird which would be extinct if it were not for its toothed beak, which among mountain people is called "the Bolt Cutter." One must, however, be notably careless, or surprised while asleep, to fall victim to this bird, since it is very slow and unable to catch a human. It prefers to look for food in the undergrowth, above all rodents and small goblins.

Call of the Flying Fell Dog

The Gatherer Troll

If there were more Gatherer Trolls, then littering in the mountains would not be a problem. Almost all trolls collect valuable objects, but a few individuals lack such criteria and collect everything they find. Perhaps they are aesthetes in their way, who can see the merits of a glass jar which has contained sliced beetroots, and of a lost camping knife of the best quality. Nor do they hesitate to pick up sweet wrappers or worn-out shoelaces. Gatherer Trolls attach no prestige whatsoever to the value of the objects. But they love their discoveries and are prepared to go to any lengths to defend their collections.

The Gatherer Troll's cave is consequently a hodgepodge of utensils and playthings from recent decades or centuries. Skins and furs jostle with modern functional garments. Asthma inhalers and invaluable Stone Age remains share a carton in a corner. Yes, a cave like that is a dream for any archaeologist. Sometimes a poor mountain hiker happens to drop into the gathering sack, finally ending up in the cave. Once one is in a gathering sack, it is tricky to get out. Even if another hiker sees your plight and sneaks forward to open the sack, the rescuer finds that the sack is fastened with an impossible knot. The Gordian knot is childishly simple in comparison.

Rope experts consider troll knots among the most difficult to untie. It is in fact almost easier to instead save someone from a Gatherer Troll's cave, if it has been located. True, the gateway to such a cave is without exception guarded by some kind of formula, but a little dynamite usually gets round that.

The Creeping Sledgehammer Troll

When hiking in the mountains and bumping into life forms, there is always uncertainty about whether what one meets has friendly intentions or not. With the Creeping Sledgehammer Troll, any such deliberations are unnecessary. It is always bent on murder, and has a sledgehammer arm ready to swing. Despite its relative smallness, just a man's height although broad as a barn door, the Creeping Sledgehammer Troll is classed a strong 3 on the Bauer scale. This troll treads lightly and creeps up on unsuspecting victims, letting the hammer fall at considerable speed. No creature is safe. The Creeping Sledgehammer Troll's negligible intelligence means that it attacks everything within swinging distance. Gnomes are a favorite prey, as with many other trolls. There is often minced gnome on the Creeping Sledgehammer Troll's table, since any other method of preparation is made more difficult by a direct hit.

Fortunately, a Creeping Sledgehammer Troll cannot make itself invisible. That is why it has been forced to refine its creeping properties.

Handle of
grip-friendly
dwarf birch.
The hammer-
head weighs
around
13 kilos.

Troll-gnome relations

These are two beings which have fundamentally and genuinely detested each other since prehistoric times. Of course trolls certainly like gnomes, either boiled with potatoes or sautéed on both sides. Lightly simmered gnome in onion soup is also considered a culinary delight. There is no real limit to trolls' creativity when it comes to tormenting gnomes. On the next page some abominable phenomena are illustrated. Luckily, gnomes are much more cunning than trolls, so it is unusual for them to be caught.

Gnome rolling: The troll rolls the gnome between the palms of its hands until the gnome staggers about uncontrollably, ignorant of which way is up or down. The troll amuses itself with this until it tires of it and throws the gnome into the pot or the frying pan.

Gnome rounders: A subtly cruel sport or game where the trolls beat the gnomes between each other with clubs. Gnomes are tough and strong and can in certain cases grab a branch or be saved by a bird, so trolls who are careful with their food do not play this game.

Trolls love to brush gnome hair with a horsehair brush. Gnomes are careful about their hairdo and they are outraged when their hair becomes disordered. They are extremely vain, even when waiting to be cooked.

Trolls often use old railway sleepers and rail spikes to make simple clubs for gnome hunting.

To add a perspective to my examples, it should be added that trolls too meet their end, or are incapacitated, by covert gnome traps. In precarious situations, gnomes can even secrete a substance similar to adrenaline, which is called gnomeine, which multiplies the gnomes' already appreciable bodily strength.

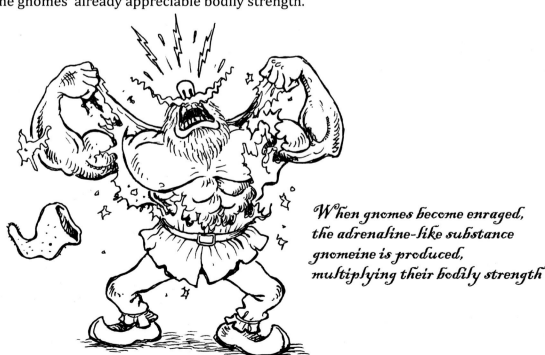

When gnomes become enraged, the adrenaline-like substance gnomeine is produced, multiplying their bodily strength

Gnome rolling

Height relationship, gnome/troll

300cm

30cm

Gnome rounders

Horsehair brushing

Railway sleeper with rail spikes

39

The Thespian Mousseron
(Teatralica musseronis)

Edible but lethal. This mushroom species captivates people with dramatic theatrical performances. They listen, initially surprised, then are carried away by the voices from the undergrowth, and forget to eat and drink. Finally, unless able to break the spell, they end their days among the mushroom colony.

Piles of bones bleaching in the sun remind us of the dangers of excessive poetry listening. The Thespian Mousseron prefers to recite Shakespeare and other authors from the late Middle Ages. Now, you cannot wander around in the mountains wearing headphones: you would miss much of the experience of nature, but it can be a good idea to be on the alert for dramatic declamations from groves of trees.

Mousseron noisette with reindeer suovas, potato purée, and lingonberry jam is a delicacy

The Screechwort, aka Roarflower

The old proverb "If the Screechwort gives you the chills, stay where you are in the hills" should be taken with a pinch of salt. This plant is stationary, and as long as you keep a respectful distance, there is no risk of injury. If perhaps you are tired of life as such and can think of nothing better to do than end your days, then by all means step up and pat this cute plant. In an instant it will bury a row of teeth in your flesh and not let go until hell freezes over. It is not one of Sweden's seven traditional Midsummer flowers...

The Sticky Hair Bolete

This mushroom has a disadvantageous appearance. But do not be deterred! It makes a gutsy dish whose consistency and flavor are like pasta. If you can bear the ugly physiognomy while cooking it, you will be rewarded with a tasty lunch rich in nutrition.

The Fleet-Footed Mushroom

A gastronomic delight. The truffle of the North, as they say in the mountains. Since it is much sought after, it has developed mobility and can when necessary quickly change its growing site. If you see a troll with a bag net creeping in the terrain, it is quite probably hunting the Fleet-Footed Mushroom.

The Gorm Troll

Sometimes you can find small throne-like dolmens on the middle of a bare mountain. These have puzzled hikers for years. If you encounter one, you can be sure that a Gorm Troll has been there. These unbearable little chieftains build their thrones, dress in regal clothing, complete with crown and scepter, and proclaim their sovereignty over an area of on average 100 m in circumference, where the throne is at the center. Gorm Trolls see it as vital to be able to survey their territory without difficulty, which is why a greater area would simply be difficult to manage.

They repeatedly practice their regal mannerisms, in particular looking superior. This is manifested by always having their noses pointing skyward. The Gorm Troll puts great store in leaning his head back as far as possible without the crown sliding off. It strives for an optimum angle of 89°. An angle of 90° is considered impossible by even the most devoted of them. A Gorm Troll thus devotes much of the day to finding this point of balance. Yes, and to looking gormlessly at everyone entering their domain without showing due respect, of course. Hence the name.

The ideal angle

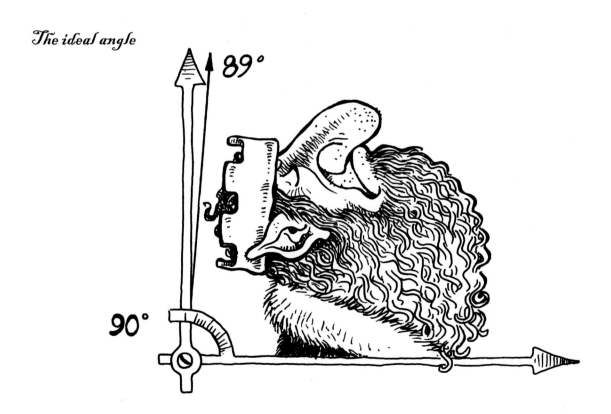

89°

90°

Scepter made of birch with garnet or snow quartz inlay

Crown of brass
(dwarfs' smithing)

43

The Brook Nymph

Do not be fooled by this esoteric apparition. The Brook Nymph has just one objective with its music and fluttering eyelashes, which is to pull hikers into the deep and drown them so that their souls keep her company forever in the cold waters of the brook.

Now, it is not all that easy to drown someone in a shallow brook: sometimes the struggle is so intensive that strong people manage to make it to the shore. Once anyone has escaped, the person often develops a healthy fear of water, especially the waters of the mountain jokk (brook). You will recognize such a person from the nervous way of filling a water flask.

The Brook Nymph is a fantastic musician and has mastered several instruments which are often reminiscent of each other, but are wrought by dwarves and colored by their particular and artistic nature. Her accordion has a strange keyboard which produces tones that are impossible on conventional instruments. An enterprising village musician from Erkheikki who ran into a Brook Nymph when hiking managed to draw the accordion while she was taking an afternoon nap in the spring sunshine and had a skilled accordion builder as faithfully as possible copy one. It was impossible for anyone other than the man from Erkheikki to play it, but he himself could perform the most complicated pieces apparently without effort. Success led to more success, and nowadays he plays the biggest venues in the world. Being likable and down to earth, he sometimes goes on tour in Tornedalen between international engagements. Then he often plays his own melody and lyrics entitled "The Sunbathing Brook Nymph Waltz."

The Parabol Gnome

These multicolored small gnomes can sense a sneezing ant at a distance of 500 m (in clear weather). Their favorite diet is above all the Bohemian Dumpling Bolete, since the Parabol Gnome is one of the few whose metabolism allows digestion of this mushroom.

The ears which are the most characteristic feature of this gnome are surprisingly mobile and can monitor 360 degrees around the skull without the need to turn the head. The mountain hiker and inventor Isodor Matojänkkä of Nedre Soppero developed one of the first military radar masts, modeled on the ears of the Parabol Gnome.

The gnome is never bothered by mosquitoes or midges, since the intensive ear flapping creates local thermal currents which the flying insects are unable to handle.

The gnome produces considerable amounts of earwax every day. Much of the day is spent cleaning wax out of its ears. For this purpose the Parabol Gnome always keeps a wax spoon handy.

It is worth adding that one of the secrets of the gnome's metabolism is the strong digestive acid. It can be used instead of 70% spirits of salt in chemical experiments. It is also very efficacious if one needs to etch, for example, damask knife blades.

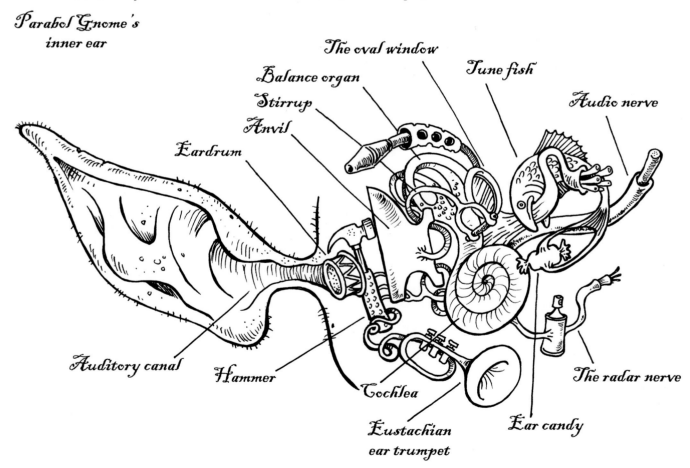

Parabol Gnome's inner ear

The oval window

Balance organ

Tune fish

Stirrup

Audio nerve

Anvil

Eardrum

Auditory canal

Hammer

Cochlea

The radar nerve

Eustachian ear trumpet

Ear candy

Daily production of earwax, 300 grams

Extremely mobile ears

Digestive acid, excellent for etching damask knife blades

Male

Female

The Globe Lightbulb Willow

Would you, dear reader, be surprised if I told you that this bush has lent its shape to the modern light bulb? This willow species is rare, but a welcome sight to the lost night hiker. The seedpods contain a gas not unlike neon which is charged during thunderstorms. The charge remains for months, but its light is only visible after nightfall. In daytime, the seedpods have a gray-white sheen not unlike that of pennycress. It cannot be a coincidence that Abisko-born Jopert Laiskasaapha, who emigrated to America, actually worked as an assistant in Thomas Alva Edison's laboratory ... once upon a time.

The Signpost Bush

This bush has its habitat at the foot of Mount Skerfe in the Rapa Valley. As far as the author knows, it is the only one in existence. There is a legend that there was a troll woman long ago who was renowned for her indecision. No matter what decision was on the cards, the woman could not make up her mind.

She was nevertheless much consulted in the region for mixing concoctions which might cure this and that. In her best moments she was skilled in this craft, alongside her ability to see into the future.

Who would dare to consult an indecisive concoction brewer, asks a stickler for order? Well, once the troll woman had drunk a cup of coffee, all hesitancy was swept away. The caffeine collected her spiritual powers into a concentrate of intense focus. Coffee was expensive in the past, so someone wishing to buy a salve, for example for gout, would be sure to bring along a bag of coffee when visiting the old woman. She would gulp down the java and mix a top-rate cream of lingonberry twigs, dried Slurry-Gravel Agaric, and massaged reindeer lichen. Everything was hunky-dory, and the woman enjoyed helping her neighbors and drinking coffee.

But one day there was a knock on the door and the local scoundrel, a member of the Creeping Sledgehammer clan, asked for a salve for a fresh knife wound from a recent skirmish. He had no coffee with him but thought the woman might mix something together anyway.

The salve was certainly effectual, but instead of healing the wound, the salve gave the troll a light and beautiful soprano voice. This was disastrous for the troll, since his normal deep bass voice was an asset when trading insults and hissing threats.

So he killed the old woman on the spot. Creeping Sledgehammers are rough types.

After a few years, the Signpost Bush grew up on the old woman's grave. It was an extension of her indecision, and so the hand-like outgrowths point in every direction.

But what few people know is that if a hiker pours fresh-brewed coffee over the bush, all the hands point simultaneously in the direction to be taken.

Troll Hunters

Sometimes a large troll, perhaps at level 5 on the Bauer scale, can start causing problems in the mountains. The troll may have developed a taste for human flesh or just feel like trashing a mountain station or demolishing a reindeer corral. That is the time to call in the County Administrative Board TAG (Trolls and Goblins) team. This is a small secret section with just a few members which was set up at the beginning of the last century to protect railway workers building the Ore Line. They were pioneers in building robots, originally steam driven, to meet danger at an early stage to secure iron ore shipments. Today they are seldom called out but are still required to go into action now and then. The robot on the opposite page is a generation 23 fully armed antitroll artillery piece manufactured by SMI (Saittarova Mechanical Industries), which incidentally has provided all the robots for the TAG team since its foundation. On the picture, the 100 hours' service is being carried out outside the workshop in the village. The robot in question is of a technical level equivalent to an advanced jet fighter. It has a crew of four, and the command station is embedded in the upper thorax. The robot contains a minimum of computer software, since certain trolls have the magic and telepathic capability to wage electronic warfare. Mechanically, however, it is well developed and resilient.

The robot on this page is a smaller variant which is sent in against trolls of up to level 3.

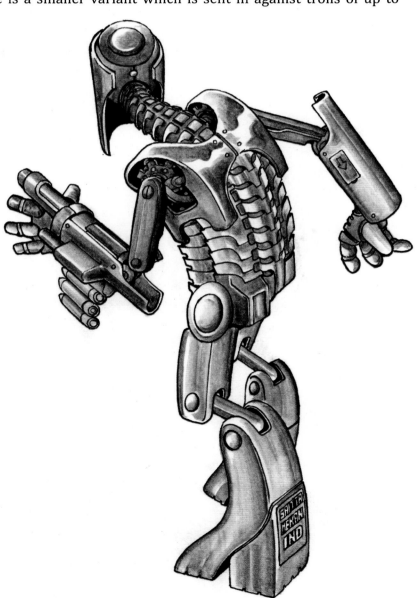

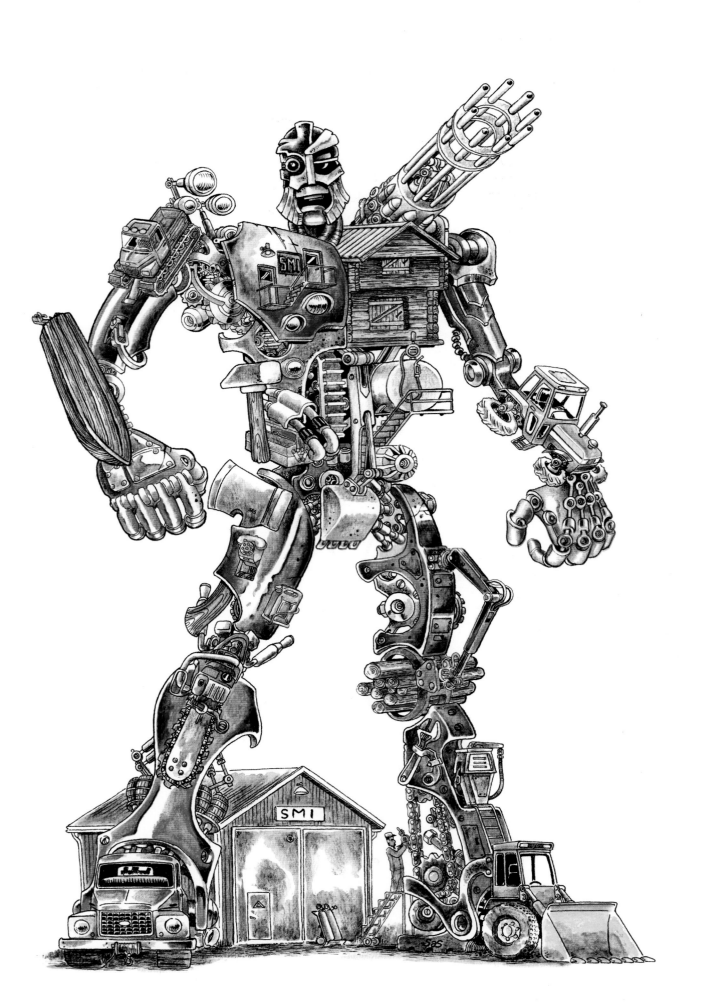

The Twelves

A few centuries ago, a clan of elves in Örkelljunga moved up to the mountains around Abisko. It was due to a family feud that got out of hand, and a breakaway group considered there could not be too great a distance between them and their antagonists. They thus decided to travel north, intending to live near the North Pole. But they modified their plans in the Abisko area as winter approached. When they were then struck by the beauty of the landscape, they made it their permanent habitat.

They call themselves Twelves (Truly Wonderful Elves) since they consider themselves to be one step above other elves. The Twelves Elves do not lack self-confidence in any way and consider that they are beyond doubt the pinnacle of creation.

The only mountain inhabitant whose character is anywhere near the grandiose and jumped-up nature of the Twelves Elves is the Gorm Troll.

The human eye perceives a Twelves Elf as merely a few black dashes

The Carnivorous Drypine

A tired and freezing hiker can often find it hard to find fuel for a campfire. Above the tree line it is practically impossible. If you then happen to run into a dry pine up on a bare mountain, it can be tempting to bury your axe in it. But beware! It is quite likely a double-crossing chameleon in woody guise known as the Carnivorous Drypine. Its plans have nothing to do with fueling a campfire.

Now, to people it is not dangerous in the sense of lethal. It lives mainly on small birds and rodents. But it defends itself vigorously against all attacks on its trunk and branches, and can cause considerable injury to those unprepared. The root system extensions can be compared to the tentacles of an octopus.

They are useful to the Drypine during severe mountain storms, when the Drypine can grip the terrain to avoid being felled by the wind.

The Drypine is perhaps the only survivor of its species. Its origin is unknown, but like so many other strange beings in the mountains, one can suspect that sorcery has played a part in its creation.

The Crawling Chopping Block

It is frightening to see at dusk, when like a giant spider it creeps over a hilltop with an axe buried in its head. It was a fully grown Carnivorous Drypine until the beginning of the 20th century, when a group of freezing and determined workers almost succeeded in sawing it up for firewood. It managed to flee when the workers had gone to bed, and since then has wandered aimlessly over the mountains, hunting for its lost trunk.

The Drypine can coordinate
its root system in a fantastic
way and effortlessly
catch up with a human

The root system also proves its
worth during severe
mountain storms

An abominable sight to a
sorely tried mountain hiker

Vidvartid Gurt

This troll, which the attentive reader will certainly recognize from the book cover, can represent the archetypal troll of the northern mountains.

Name: Vidvartid Gurt
Home area: west of Björkliden
Age: approx. 308 years
Height: 3.40 m
Weight: 310 kg
Bauer scale: a strong 3

Physical and spiritual qualities:

Gurt has good hearing, as do all trolls, perhaps with the exception of certain Hair Trolls. Eyesight? Gurt's small, sly eye slits correctly indicate poor eyesight, but seldom has one experienced more ominous staring than from this pair of yellow eyes. Gurt is blessed with a predatory grin with pointed teeth where the corners of the mouth remarkably often point downward, revealing a destructive and dark view of existence.

Sense of smell: The large nose has sensitive receptors which can detect potential prey from far off. It is then useless to pretend to be a statue and hope that the troll's poor eyesight will save you. Be aware of the wind direction when encountering dangerous trolls.

Gurt's tail is an excellent indicator of his current mood. If it is pointing straight up, he is particularly furious. The more it is lowered, the angrier he is becoming. Quite simply, Gurt is consistent in his moods — they are always bad.

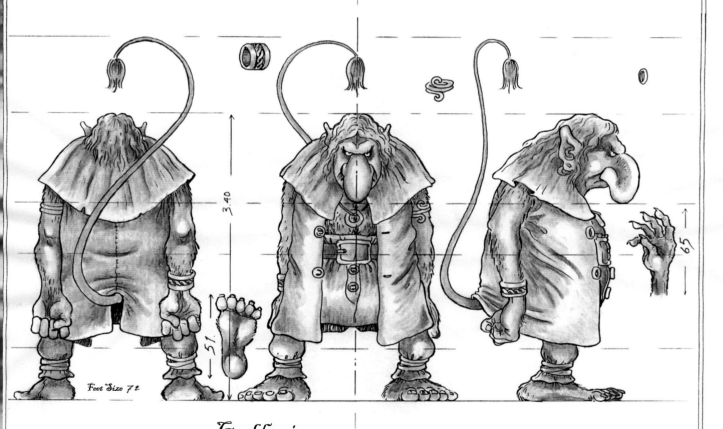

Feet Size 7½

Good hearing

Evil eyes

Wear-resistant fangs

Abnormal nose

The Saber-Toothed Reindeer
(Rangifer tupplaveittius)

The pointed antlers and the long saber-like fangs, alongside innate aggressive behavior, are all good reasons to make a detour around this reindeer.

So how has this reindeer been gifted with these frightening attributes? The origin is in the misty past, but there is a verbal tradition, told around campfires, that in the past a Sami community spent generations single-mindedly and industriously breeding them in order to create a weapon strong enough to protect reindeer herds from predators. It was successful for a long time. But the aggressiveness and love of freedom of the Saber-Toothed Reindeer took over, and one night they all escaped from their corral and since then have been living on the mountain. It is a small but hardy population which sometimes infiltrates ordinary reindeer herds, but usually wanders alone in high valleys.

The Snowman

Very little is known about the Scandinavian Snowman. He is one of many phenomena which are invisible to the naked eye. Occult spectacles are required, with a maximum wavelength spectrum. More about these spectacles later. However, the testimony that can be considered credible has it that the Snowman, despite its appearance, is not particularly dangerous or aggressive if one keeps a respectful distance of 100 m.

Anyone who approaches nearer is, without exception, torn to pieces amid terrifying roars.

Headless Trolls

"How is this even possible?" the bookish biologist will naturally wonder. Yes, these academic theoreticians sometimes find it difficult to understand certain phenomena in nature. Naturally, the Headless Trolls consider that a temporary relocation of the head below the arm is the most natural thing in the world and consider themselves somewhat more refined than the ordinary troll.

The advantages of a detachable head are many, as illustrated here; besides, the fearsome effect upon mountain hikers should not be underestimated. There are disadvantages of course, as illustrated on the next page. These trolls have given rise to a number of sayings, such as "running around like a Headless Troll" or acting as though one has "one's troll head in the sand."

The well-known electronic engineer Astor Brehmerfelte of Stuttgart, who was also an avid mountain hiker, visited these parts in the beginning of the 80s, and ran into a troll of the headless type. He was of course frightened, but his professional side took over and he studied and drew far-reaching conclusions about wireless communications and later developed methods leading to today's digital wireless networks. Trolls do not, of course, use the same laws of physics as two communicating digital units, but Astor claims that it was then and there the idea arose.

Troll running around like a headless chicken

Headless Trolls

A sight in truth scary to the nervous mountain hiker...

Troll who has happened to put his head on backward

It can be disastrous for the troll to put its head down... The body can walk away...

Bone troll comb

For apparent reasons, these trolls have a good overview

2 on the scale!

The headless often stick together!

The Mine Dwarfs

This illustrious company of Mine Dwarfs are on their way to their mine at the foot of Kebnekaise. They are all in the grip of a kind of chronic gold fever and cannot quite get enough of the yellow metal. It is true they also extract other things too: other metals, minerals, and beautiful rock types.

But gold holds a special place among dwarfs. They could quite easily carry on mining around the clock if it were not for the fact that like earthly life forms in general, they need to eat, drink, and rest from time to time.

The dwarf women, however, are indifferent to mining. They are totally uninterested in pickaxes, tunneling, and eruptive minerals. They much prefer heavy cannons and calculating the ballistic trajectory of gunpowder-propelled projectiles. They often sit perched on hills, monitoring the surroundings with their artillery and a stock of shells. For this reason, Creeping Sledgehammers, Flying Fell Dogs, Saber-Toothed Reindeer, and other roughnecks hesitate to approach dwarf dwellings.

Weapon care and maintenance

The Viper Fern

A toxic, fast-attacking plant of the fern family. Its 5 heads emanate from a single body. Just like with the mythological monster the Hydra, a severed head grows back again. This can be nerve racking if one does not know about it and is in the middle of a life-or-death struggle. The fern has long been known as a medicinal plant, and the only way to harvest it is to chop off the stem near the root. The stem is almost wooden, and it takes a few swings of the axe. When you hear a long-drawn-out bellow of doom, followed by a fading hiss, you know the plant is safe to carry away. Just look out for the death throes. If you are bitten, lie absolutely still, so that the toxin does not spread in your blood as quickly.

The Bubble Bush

A highly epicurean plant. The stem is often artistically twisted like a well-kept bonsai tree, and the blue tone of the soap bubble-like seedpods gives the plant an almost extraterrestrial appearance. When the growing season approaches, the seed dispersal is a memorable spectacle. The seedpods release themselves from the twigs and then float away, sometimes a good distance, before they ultimately burst like a housing bubble. The liquid in the bubbles is slightly acidic, to the same degree as 12% spirits of salt.

The Viper Fern

Bubble Bush

65

The Tarfala Gnome

One might think that many mountain hikers might be inquisitive about the little oval door in the hill on the left side of the trail leading to Tarfala, shortly after one leaves Láddjujávri.

But the door is under an uninterestedness spell cast by the trolls in the region. If you go close you can see something reminiscent of runic lettering, although the font is a little rounder. If you persist and walk down the stairs, you come to a gigantic machine room. The gnomes in this area have a well-developed interest in technology and spend all their waking hours honing their skills in diverse mechanical projects. But it is perhaps still surprising to hear that they are behind such advanced innovations as the switch-inductive velodrome steam boiler or the centrifugal brake seismograph.

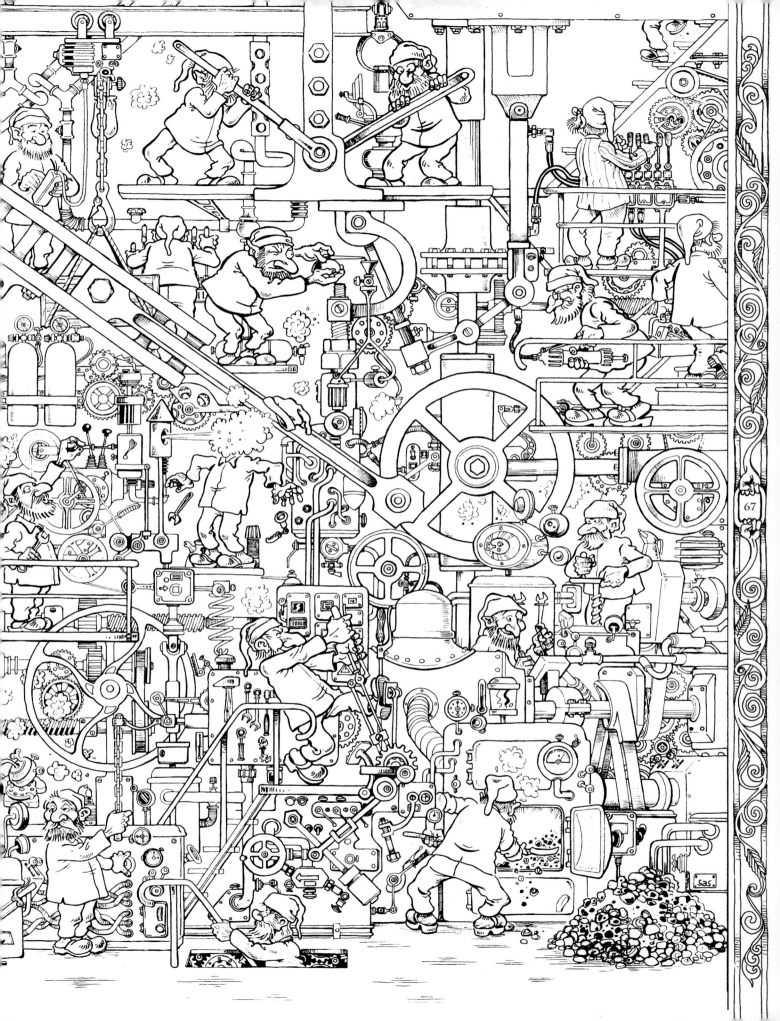

Occult spectacles

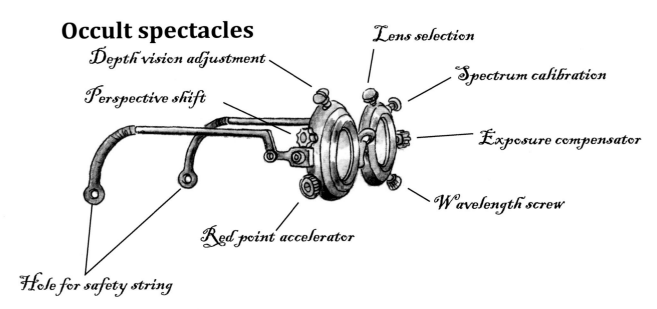

Lens selection

Depth vision adjustment

Spectrum calibration

Perspective shift

Exposure compensator

Wavelength screw

Red point accelerator

Hole for safety string

As suggested earlier, many trolls and beings have an ability to make themselves dark or completely invisible to people who appear within their field of vision. This smacks of unfairness, and gives the trolls a clear advantage. The solution is occult-formula spectacles. They are made of quartz dredged from the bottom of Trollsjön (Troll Lake). Troll quartz reaches its maximum magic capacity in the coldest nights of January, so it is not easy to find divers willing to force their way through 3 m of ice while avoiding waking up the constantly hungry giant ray which slumbers in the benthic gravel and to try not to freeze to death in the icy water.

It goes without saying that the spectacles are expensive once they have been raised, transported to the Kristallen stone polishing center in Lannavaara for sawing, polishing, and mounting, and sent on to the only optician in the country who markets this unique product. But there are few who know where this shop, which opened as early as 1898, is located, and that is for a very good reason. Trade in occult spectacles is forbidden, and from its early days the shop has kept a low profile.

The picturesque little square Meschplan in Kiruna is where the trade flourishes. The cafés, bookshops, and clothes shops surround a clump of birch trees, a bench, and a shallow little fountain. In the middle of all this commerce, there is a house wall displaying a conspicuous absence of doors and windows. No one notices it since the mustard plasterwork is not particularly exciting to the average shopper. And that is exactly how she likes it, Siv who owns Siv's Occult Opticians. It is ironic that in order to see her shop, you need a pair of occult spectacles.

MANUALE FÖR BEVÄSNINGS POLARISERADE BINOCKULARE ANNO 1898

Troll quartz

Budget monocle

View without
occult spectacles

View with
occult spectacles

SIV'S
OCCULT
OPTICIANS

23

Siv

69

Stallo

This genuinely mean and sly apparition covers vast areas. One day he is seen far down in the Tornedalen conifer belt; the next he has been seen on the Norwegian border or in Västerbotten County. It is a mystery yet unsolved how Stallo can cover these incredible distances in such a short time. The well-known physicist and son of Gällivare, Higesippus Lorgnette-Kyrötalo, launched a theory citing so-called wormholes (gaps in spacetime which enable travel at a timeless speed) when the author interviewed him a year and a half ago. I myself suspect that he is the owner of the legendary seven-league boots. Stallo often carries an enchanted axe which is razor sharp and never needs honing. It can cut through everything and adapts its size and weight to the person currently holding the handle. Down the years, many foresters have longed for this tool. More than once, Stallo has sold the axe or traded it in some shady transaction, because he knows the axe will always return to him sooner or later. Stallo is omnivorous, although vegetables are perhaps not his first-hand choice—he prefers well-built mountain hikers. Try therefore to look slim and haggard if you bump into Stallo. Cough if you can, clear your throat often. Stallo avoids people who have a cold, which gives the flesh a stale taste, in his opinion. He is, as we have said, utterly devious, and will ask after your health through cunningly formulated questions. He is not unlike an experienced telemarketer. In this case you must hang up immediately... In other words, change the subject; otherwise you will soon be swimming, bruised, in a pot together with spring vegetables and a few fistfuls of crowberries.

Luckily, Stallo cannot make himself invisible. It is apparently a cardinal rule that the bigger the trolls, the harder it is for them to make themselves invisible. Incidentally, Stallo is a 4 on the Bauer scale.

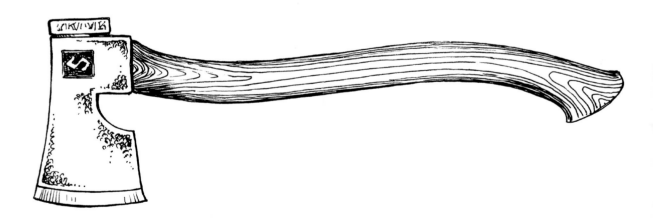

Dwarf Smiths

If the Tarfala Gnomes are the mountain dwellers who are at the cutting edge of mechanical engineering and innovative thinking, then the Dwarf Smiths of Katterjåkk are their counterparts in traditional smithing. They are specialists in iron curlicuing, tapering, tempering, riveting, welding, and artistically expressed iron twisting, to the power of ten.

A typical Dwarf Smith cannot forge a simple pair of tongs without embellishing it in some way. To leave an iron surface untouched he considers ridiculous. Of course, this makes every workpiece infinitely more complex than necessary, but it is a cross he must bear, as this smith would put it.

The working environment of the Dwarf Smith is illustrated on the opposite side. In the picture, the Skerfe Troll has come to get a new hinge for his dwelling hole. The old one simply fell off the door after just 180 years' service. This is actually good performance, since the Skerfe Troll, like trolls in general, always slams his door with a full follow-through. It is as though he is hostile to doors and hinges. Anyway, here he is sitting watching the Dwarf Smith's efforts and wondering how he can conclude this business with as little impact as possible on his own hard-earned capital.

He has already tried complaining about the old hinge, pointing out shortcomings in the curves and muttering about faulty manufacture. The dwarfs, who have well-developed professional pride and formidable hereditary self-confidence, in no way consider that any error has been committed. The stage is set for discussions when the job is done.

The Abisko Werewolf

When the tired mountain hiker has prepared an overnight camp and is lying at rest in the tent, this is probably the last being the hiker wants to be awoken by. It seems superfluous to describe the properties of the werewolf, since they have been amply presented in literature for centuries.

What distinguishes the Abisko Werewolf from its literary cousins is that it is extraordinarily difficult to liquidate. But since this is a factual book and the author is conscientious with regard to details, I shall of course present the correct procedure.

Acquire a musket handgun from the latter 1630s of the Augsbergher-Schmettelkopf brand. Load it with a silver bullet which should be cast under a full moon on a Thursday between Septuagesima and the Feast of the Annunciation. If the werewolf is shot with this bullet, from such a pistol, a favorable outcome can be guaranteed. It should of course be hit in the heart, preferably the right ventricle if possible.

To the man on the street, these criteria may make the task seem daunting. Overwhelming even. Luckily there is an alternative. One can drill through the werewolf's heart with a lance of gray alder whose tip has been sooted in a fire lit with tinder and a consecrated striking steel forged by Dwarf Smiths on a January evening in a light southeasterly breeze at the foot of Kebnekaise.

Armored Snails

The trolls' hoodlum age comes
in the early teens. In their case,
around the age of 50.

The Wirehaired
Double-Furred
Low Fell Rodent

The Stone Bellower

As all Kiruna people know, blasting takes place in the mine around 1:20 every night. A Kiruna dweller seldom or never wakes up from the sounds, hardened by decades of dull thuds. Tourists wake up of course, unless they are here in summer and are already awake due to the midnight sun.

But now and then even the most heavily snoozing native is wakened from his or her beauty sleep by an extended rustling bellow, similar to a cement mixer containing only gravel, although much louder, almost human, and always after midnight. It is clear to the ear that it is something aboveground, and those with good local knowledge can work out that the sound is coming from the piles of old waste rock deposited during more than a century of mining.

It is the Stone Bellowers, an incarnation of ethereal beings of mineral and stone who dislike being among the rock piles. Erosion regularly frees enough magic mineral for the Stone Bellowers to take form. However, it is painful for them to be reshaped into a body of stone, and they scream and bellow from the birth pangs and from despair, since they know that they are only going to live until the first hours of dawn. They set course for the mine and slowly begin to trudge back to the interior of the mountain, where they have dwelled since the earth's creation. But most do not make it, and they begin to decompose as soon as they take their first steps, and the process is quick and merciless.

This is the sole explanation for the apparently randomly distributed small heaps of gravel one can suddenly run into in the middle of a housing area in Kiruna.

Who came first?

Well, this is a burning political issue. But as a conscientious author I must not evade the charged topic. So how does the historical perspective look? How were the mountains populated by trolls in the misty past? I put the question, of course, to the ancient Vistavagge Troll.

"Ehuuummmm..." (He always starts like that; I believe he is clearing his troll throat, a deafening sound.)

"When the inland ice retreated, two tribes invaded. The Mammoth-Riding Wild Trolls came from the east, and the Hotheaded Spear Trolls came from the south.

"It was not long before full-scale war broke out between these groups. The Wild Trolls relied on brute strength and determination, and always attacked uncompromisingly with full force and vulgar insults with their mammoths and double clubs. The Spear Trolls, for their part, used cunning and tactics, mostly because they had no mammoths. They stood for innovation on the battlefield, as with the tandem-powered pincer maneuver, the bouncing flanking prowl, and the supported Čakkeli press. Hard fighting continued for centuries until the tribes made peace on the island of Entaisteleennäsaari on Lake Torneträsk in 304 AD (human dating system)."

The Clump Nymph

The Clump Nymphs do not possess the ability to make themselves invisible, but they are nigh impossible to detect among the clumps of Carex cespitosa sedge in the border zone between land and water. This nymph is related to the Forest Nymph and shares its inclination to make trouble for people. It enjoys nothing better than showering oaths over some poor mountain angler or reindeer herd. Caution is essential here. Do not trample around among the sedge clumps, for if you happen across a Clump Nymph you can be sure that you have caught your last Arctic char. You will not be liquidated on the spot, but will suffer under a lifelong curse that makes the fish stop biting forever.

On the other hand, a resourceful and enterprising angler can make a sacrifice to the Clump Nymphs—they love that. Leave a good-quality spool reel or a freshly landed Arctic char on a clump near a population of Clump Nymphs and you will see that your success at angling will reach new levels. But it is risky, a little like Tjuonavagge roulette with Mora knives. But that is another story.

Clump Nymphs are a beautiful sight. It is a fact that the expression "a clump in my throat" comes from a Swedish poet who happened to see a picture of a Clump Nymph and was extremely taken. According to sources, the expression "a little sedge can break the reindeer's back" comes from an occasion when a gieres sleigh fully laden with iron bars took a shortcut across a field of Carex cespitosa sedge and later had to take the consequences for this hooliganism.

A surprisingly large number of Swedish sayings, then, originate in the world of mountain mythology!

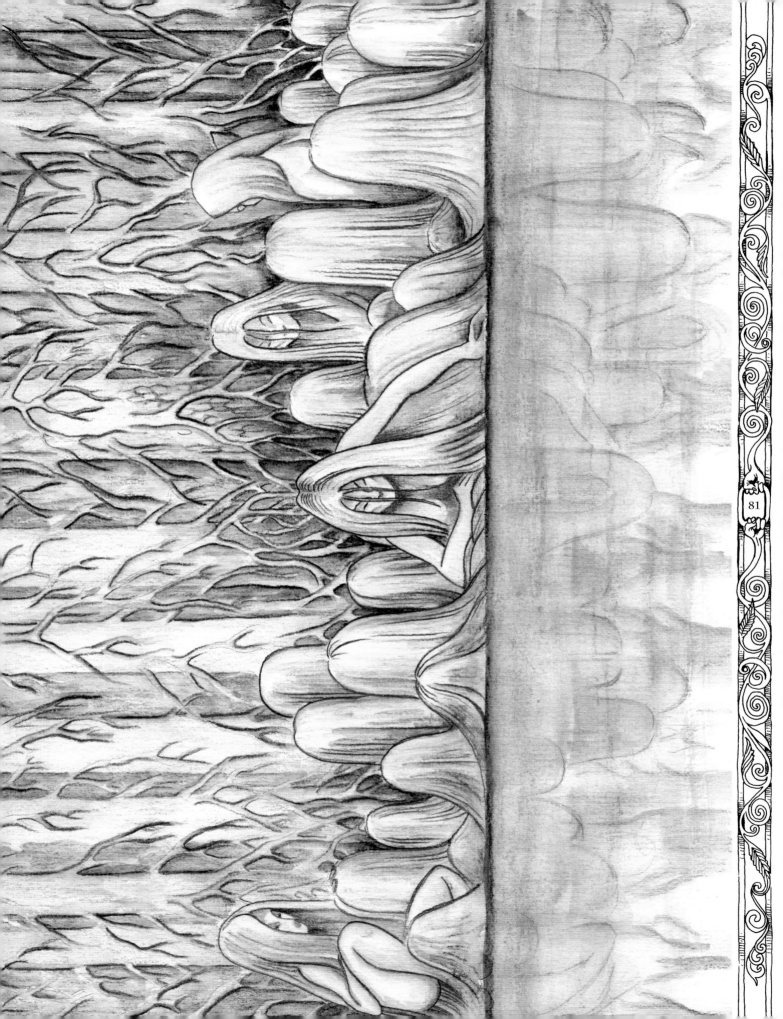

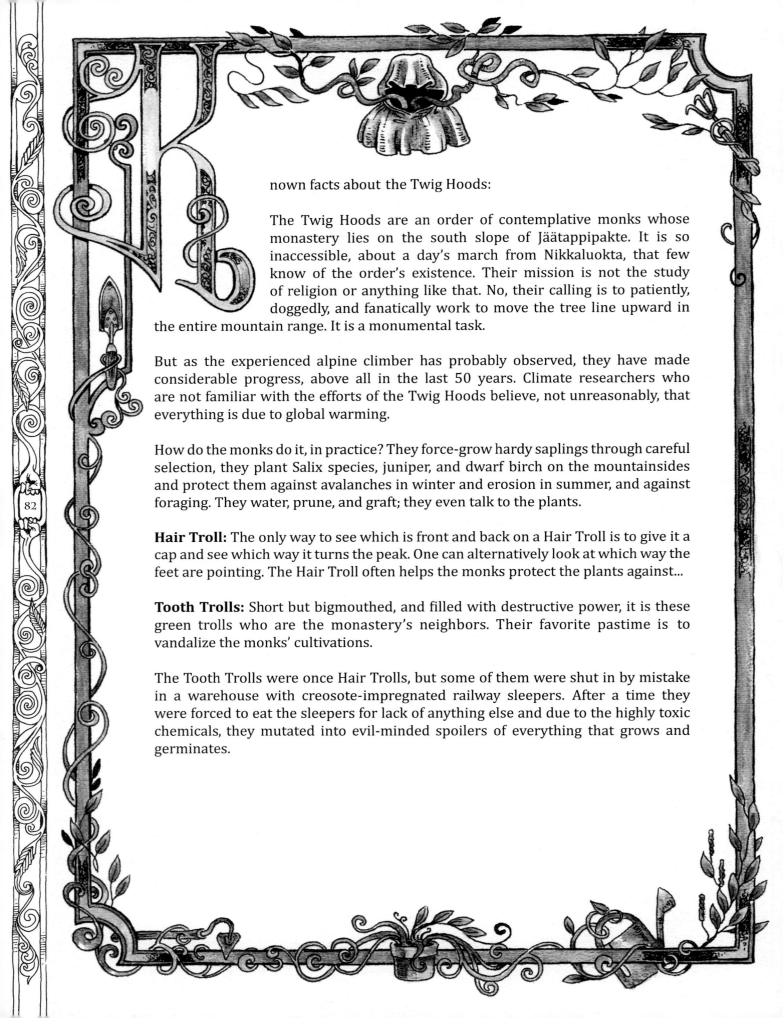

nown facts about the Twig Hoods:

The Twig Hoods are an order of contemplative monks whose monastery lies on the south slope of Jäätappipakte. It is so inaccessible, about a day's march from Nikkaluokta, that few know of the order's existence. Their mission is not the study of religion or anything like that. No, their calling is to patiently, doggedly, and fanatically work to move the tree line upward in the entire mountain range. It is a monumental task.

But as the experienced alpine climber has probably observed, they have made considerable progress, above all in the last 50 years. Climate researchers who are not familiar with the efforts of the Twig Hoods believe, not unreasonably, that everything is due to global warming.

How do the monks do it, in practice? They force-grow hardy saplings through careful selection, they plant Salix species, juniper, and dwarf birch on the mountainsides and protect them against avalanches in winter and erosion in summer, and against foraging. They water, prune, and graft; they even talk to the plants.

Hair Troll: The only way to see which is front and back on a Hair Troll is to give it a cap and see which way it turns the peak. One can alternatively look at which way the feet are pointing. The Hair Troll often helps the monks protect the plants against...

Tooth Trolls: Short but bigmouthed, and filled with destructive power, it is these green trolls who are the monastery's neighbors. Their favorite pastime is to vandalize the monks' cultivations.

The Tooth Trolls were once Hair Trolls, but some of them were shut in by mistake in a warehouse with creosote-impregnated railway sleepers. After a time they were forced to eat the sleepers for lack of anything else and due to the highly toxic chemicals, they mutated into evil-minded spoilers of everything that grows and germinates.

Twig Hoods

Hair Trolls

BJORK LIDEN

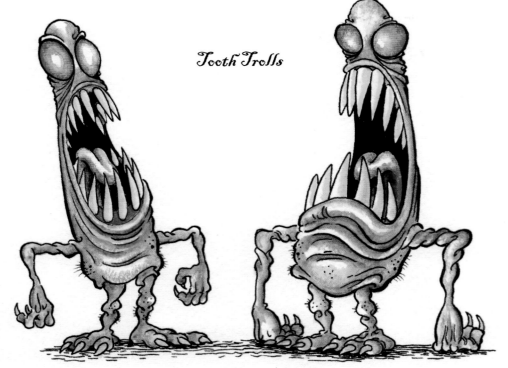

Tooth Trolls

The Saltoluokta Troll

The Saltoluokta Troll is not as dangerous as it seems at first glance. This troll does not make much of a splash when sober. Filled with alcohol, however, this troll is particularly troublesome. Mister Summer-Salt, as he is also called, probably holds his liquor worse than anyone else in the mountain world. He can summon up remarkably energetic rage and a genuine passion for vandalizing, the like of which can only be found in suburbs far to the south. He demolishes railway embankments and rips up the rails; he rampages among holiday cabins and reindeer herds. In short, he is a troublemaker when he is drunk. On occasions like this, then, naturally the County Administrative Board TAG team (see p. 50) is called out. They send in their biggest robot (Malte upgr gen 23) for the protection of life and property. The battles are usually quite lively.

The Saltoluokta Troll is especially fond of the Brewer Gnomes' strong stuff, in particular a bitter ale entirely made of natural ingredients, which has an alcohol content of 71%.

The Vassijaure Brewer Gnomes

The Vassijaure Brewer Gnomes have a mobile brewery which can be quickly set up anywhere as long as there is running water nearby. Their operations are not popular with TAG. That is the main reason why their business is mobile. Their products seem a little suspect in that the ingredients include the Nail Agaric Mushroom, Constipation Morel, and Porridge Lichen. But any doubt is dispelled once one tastes a sample. Only a negligible proportion of drinkers lose their sight or become paralyzed, and the symptoms are only temporary. Those allergic to fur should not drink this, however. No one knows why; that is just the way it is. Its preparation can look coarse and random, but the gnomes are quite familiar with the ingredients, temperature, and seasoning. The high alcohol content also makes the drink acceptable to the taste buds. It is easy to see where the gnomes' vat has stood, since a barren, sterile patch is formed about 3 m in diameter, and it takes many years for vegetation to return to the spot.

The Spotted Scorpion Frog

This life form enjoys a number of deterrent attributes. Claws, fangs, and a scorpion tail with appurtenant poison barb. It can seem that evolution has overdone things here, as you will likely agree. The only sizable population is found in Hengenvaaralinen Jaure, not far from Rautas.

The Barbed-Armor Perch

This is found in Lake Torneträsk and tastes roughly the way it looks. "There are not enough spices in the world to make this fish edible," said master chef Werner Mögel on one occasion. Whether it is true is debatable, but it is a tricky bugger to catch.

The Arctic Sea Reindeer

Is this a relative of the genus Hippocampus (seahorses)? No, the origin of this water creature can be traced to a bored Brook Nymph in ancient times. It was a time when fewer people spent time in the mountains who could be fooled into the water, so the nymph began to make plans to get some pets. So a couple of reindeer calves were pulled down into the water to be transformed into water living creatures where only the reindeer antler crown indicates their genesis. The Sea Reindeer is tasty and has given rise to the popular dish suovas sushi.

The gnome submarine

When the Abisko Gnomes want to vary their diet with some seafood, they often go fishing with the armed deep-water vessel in the picture. They were well ahead of humans in developing underwater ships, and it is not impossible that Jules Verne toured in the mountains in his youth and got the idea for the Nautilus from the Abisko Gnomes.

The Dystopic Fin Flapper

The Dystopic Fin Flapper is another tasty fish suitable for breading. Unfortunately it is seriously electric and often shocks anglers something awful.

The Leviathan Trout

To round off, the Leviathan Trout, aka the "Brook Diver's Scourge," is the uncrowned scoundrel king of mountain waters. It has no prejudices against any prey, but will avidly eat other fish as well as land-based wildlife. Remarkable objects have been found in the stomachs of landed Leviathan Trout: chainsaws, tourists from Värmland, shotguns, and waffle makers. Do not underestimate this water hazard while you are in the mountains!

The Reveille Thistle

The exterior of this plant gives the observer a few clues about its properties. In favorable winds, the characteristic Reveille Thistle bloom generates a trumpet sound of considerable volume. It is like the trumpets that once blew down the walls of Jericho. It happens when the wind coaxes the stem leaves into vibrating at a certain resonance that the sound arises. It is similar to the guttural sound produced when one drops a fist-sized stone onto an unprotected little toe (although at 180dB).

The Infernal Toadstool

More poisonous than the highly toxic Death Cap Toadstool. It grows in a small area in Sarek National Park. Some trolls cultivate the toadstool to mix into disgusting concoctions to make the surroundings around their dwellings more inhospitable, to deter animals and people from approaching.

The Sneezing Buttercup

This buttercup species stands sneezing almost all day. It is the ultranemesis of those suffering from pollen allergies and can also cause a fully functioning human breathing and smelling organ to go on strike. So make a detour if you come across a stand of these yellow-and-orange bigtime sneezers.

The Scalp Bolete

This is a really tasty mushroom. One should, however, be a totally fanatic mushroomophile to harvest these hairy mushrooms, since they are highly emotional and sensitive. If a Scalp Bolete sees a mushroom knife, its hair stands on end and the body language expresses such horror and death anguish that it feels almost impossible to cut off the body of this hairdo-obsessed organism of the saprophyte kingdom.

Eargrass

If Eargrass could speak, it might tell us a great deal about what goes on in the mountain world. This plant has hearing comparable to that of the Parabol Gnome, perhaps even better.

This is sometimes exploited by small parasitic fungi which grow near Eargrass and link their mycelia into the grass roots, thereby gaining access to its hearing apparatus. Today's computer hackers work in the same way. For obvious reasons, Eargrass is no fan of the Reveille Thistle, whose sharp siren sound is torture to all eared organisms.

Karvor Slope-Ore

It is time for a few words about Karvor Slope-Ore. The importance of this grand old man in mountain-related research is hard to overestimate. Fortunately I know him, and have had free access to his extensive library and collections. In the picture on the right he is sitting in the abovementioned library in his spacious flat on Adolf Hedinsvägen road in Kiruna.

What originally made Karvor interested in trolls and goblins? Well, as a newly qualified geologist, he hiked up in the mountains to prospect for minerals, metals, and gems.

In the first week, after almost being drowned by a Brook Nymph, poisoned by a Cramp Agaric Mushroom, chased by a Predatory Hare, and thoroughly beaten by a Creeping Sledgehammer, Karvor realized that more knowledge about the new environment would not be amiss.

He eventually understood that he should approach the new flora and fauna with respect and caution, and after some years his newly awoken interest took more and more time from his prospecting. Soon he was employed by TAG as a troll researcher, and his work has led to much greater understanding of the troll environment in the mountains.

Over the years, despite his relative caution, Karvor has been bitten and poisoned by more or less every toxic plant, flower, or animal with a habitat in this barren part of the world. He has survived everything and along the way become immune to many of them. One can only admire such a painstaking interest and devotion to science.

Karvor sitting in his library on Adolf Hedinsvägen

Some that did not find space in the descriptive text

Sometimes the Bauer scale
is inadequate...

93

Do not forget to pack...

Consecrated Dwarf Smith striking steel.
Preferably made of Kirunavaara ore.

A pair of occult spectacles
from Siv's opticians,
in a sturdy case.

Spirit-calibrated compass.
On sale at Jokkmokk Market
at the handicraft stall
near the crossing.

Troll cross reinforced by
turning. Hung from
a strong leather strap.

Musket handgun from
1630 of the Augsbergher-
Schmettelkopf brand,
and some silver bullets.

Earplugs against
Roarflower,
Reveille Thistle,
Flying Fell Dog, etc., etc.

Literature such as the manual for
Siv's spectacles, a rune translator, and
The Troll Guide.

My warm thanks to:

Kent, for professionally scanning the pictures. And for talks about world events, knife crafting, and the flycatcher's nesting periods. You can cover a lot while the pictures are being fed in.

Andreas, for wanting to publish the book, for nice typesetting, and for good cooperation.

Paul, for translating the book into English.

Emelie and **Sarah**, for proofreading the text material.

Karvor, for free access to the occult library on Adolf Hedinsvägen, for lending the spectacles, and for testimony about the important parts of the mountain world.

The Vistavagge Troll, for the historical aspects and because it is always nice to have a chat on the way into the valley.

Some warned me of the risk of being altered by working on this type of book for a long time. A strange thing to say. I for one have not noticed anything...

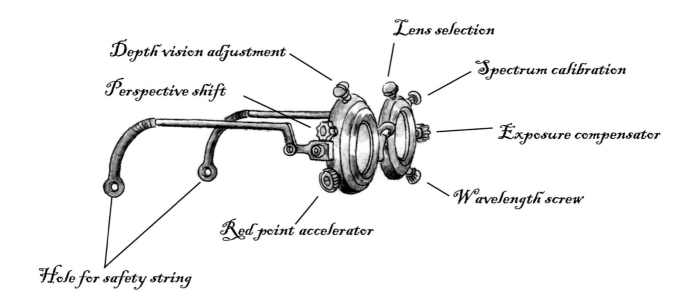

Lens selection

Depth vision adjustment

Spectrum calibration

Perspective shift

Exposure compensator

Wavelength screw

Red point accelerator

Hole for safety string

THE MAN WHO LIVES AMONG THE TROLLS

Anders Skoglind, the Swedish artist and writer of *The Troll Guide*, lives and works as a comic artist in his studio in Kiruna, in northern Sweden. But there are many days when he simply disappears, and the light in his studio stays dark.

Very few people know that Anders spends much of his time in the wilderness of Sweden, where he has a blacksmith shop on his family's old farm. And there, in a wilderness inhabited, according to legend, by trolls, Anders makes his beautiful axes. Tourists from all over the world buy Anders's axes, which perfectly fit into their backpacks, before heading into the deep forests in search of the elusive trolls.

The Troll Guide is born from the folklore of the wilderness Anders lives in.

Troll quartz

Budget monocle

While Anders works with many blacksmithing tools, the foundation of his craft is the hot iron with the trinity of hammer, anvil, and forge.

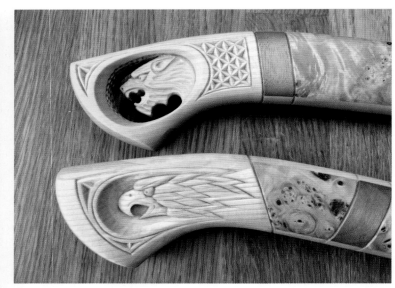

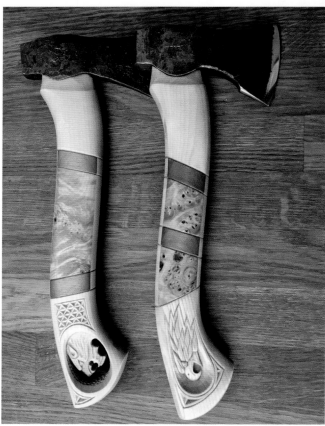

Useful, attractive, and sophisticated. These are some of the intricate designs Anders is known for.

president & publisher
Mike Richardson

collection editor
Judy Khuu

translator
Paul Fischer

collection designer
Brennan Thome

digital art technician
Adam Pruett

Special thanks to Kent Tunlind, Andreas Eriksson, Emelie Hedlund, Sarah Fahlesson, Karvor Släntmalm, Ervin Rustemagić, and Jemiah Jefferson.

THE TROLL GUIDE

Published by Dark Horse Books
A division of Dark Horse Comics LLC
10956 SE Main Street
Milwaukie, OR 97222

DarkHorse.com
SAFComics.com

Library of Congress Cataloging-in-Publication Data

Names: Skoglind, Anders, author.
Title: The troll guide / by Anders Skoglind.
Description: Milwaukie, OR : Dark Horse Books, [2020] | Summary: "This
    essential handbook is filled with tips and tricks on what to do when
    encountering trolls, as well as a comprehensive list of the different
    kinds of trolls and mountain creatures"-- Provided by publisher.
Identifiers: LCCN 2020018668 | ISBN 9781506716640 (paperback)
Subjects: LCSH: Trolls.
Classification: LCC GR555 .S64 2020 | DDC 398.21--dc23
LC record available at https://lccn.loc.gov/2020018668

First English Edition: October 2020
ISBN: 978-1-50671-664-0

1 3 5 7 9 10 8 6 4 2
Printed in China

WESTERN NOIR FROM LEGENDARY COMICS CREATOR JOE KUBERT!

A compelling adventure tale of a young man growing up during the time of the Industrial Revolution and World War I. After the murder of his family and being left for dead by robber barons, Abraham Stone travels across America in search of a fresh start in life.

$19.99 / ISBN 978-1-50671-662-6

A BRAND-NEW EDITION OF THE GREATEST WORK FROM COMICS MASTER JOE KUBERT!

The astonishing true story of a family in Sarajevo, Bosnia, trapped in a city under siege as war and genocide rage around them, with only a fax machine to communicate. A tale of hope, promise, and survival amidst mass tragedy.

$19.99 / ISBN 978-1-50671-663-3

Available at your local comics shop or bookstore! To find a comics shop in your area, visit comicshoplocator.com | For more information or to order direct, visit DarkHorse.com

Welcome to Rocavarancolia.

Welcome to the Kingdom of wonder and fright, of monsters and nightmares. Welcome to a Kingdom at death's door.

After a long, hard-fought war, Rocavarancolia languishes, a city in ruins. There are no more dragons in the skies; vampires are dying of thirst; and magic is but a pale reflection of what it used to be.

Twelve teenagers from around the world are pulled into this mystical realm of devastation and cruelty. Here, they must survive until the Red Moon rises, hardly an easy feat. For the last thirty years, no one has ever made it. Death awaits in every shadow and Rocavarancolia has no mercy, no place, for the weak.

The first volume in the young-adult dark fantasy trilogy that took Europe by storm has arrived on our shores!

$14.99 / ISBN 978-1-50671-680-0

THE CYCLE OF THE
RED MOON

BOOK ONE
THE HARVEST OF
SAMHEIN

JOSÉ ANTONIO COTRINA